Francesca Simon

Interior illustrations by **Tony Ross**

L. A. F. :)
Books

Hyperion Books for Children
New York

First published in the United States in 1999.
First published in Great Britain by Orion Children's Books in 1994.
First published in paperback by Orion Children's Books in 1995.
Text copyright ©1994 by Francesca Simon
Illustrations copyright ©1994 by Tony Ross
For information address Hyperion Paperbacks for Children,
114 Fifth Avenue, New York, New York 10011-5690.

First American Edition
1 3 5 7 9 10 8 6 4 2

Library of Congress Cataloging-in-Publication Data
Simon, Francesca.
Horrid Henry/by Francesca Simon; illustrated by Tony Ross—1st
American ed.
p. cm.
Summary: Horrid Henry causes his brother Perfect Peter all sorts
of problems when he behaves properly for a change, upstages
Peter at a dance recital, plays pirates, and goes on a camping trip.
ISBN 0-7868-1367-9 (pbk.)—ISBN 0-7868-2451-4 (lib. ed.)
[1. Behavior—Fiction. 2. Brothers—Fiction.] I. Ross, Tony, ill. II. Title.
PZ7.S604Ho 1999
[Fic]—dc21 98-54208

For Joshua and his friends
Dominic, Eleanor,
Freddie, Harry, Joe,
Robbie, and Toby
with love

CONTENTS

Chapter 1

HORRID HENRY'S PERFECT DAY

Henry was horrid.

Everyone said so, even his mother.

Henry threw food, Henry snatched, Henry pushed and shoved and pinched. Even his teddy bear avoided him when possible.

His parents despaired.

"What are we going to do about that horrid boy?" sighed Mom.

"How did two people as nice as us have such a horrid child?" sighed Dad.

When Horrid Henry's parents took Henry to school they walked behind him and pretended he was not theirs.

Children pointed at Henry and whispered to their parents, "That's Horrid Henry."

"He's the boy who threw my jacket in the mud."

"He's the boy who squashed Billy's beetle."

"He's the boy who . . ." Fill in whatever terrible deed you like. Horrid Henry was sure to have done it.

Horrid Henry had a younger brother. His name was Perfect Peter.

Perfect Peter always said "Please" and "Thank you." Perfect Peter loved vegetables.

Perfect Peter always used a tissue and never, ever picked his nose.

"Why can't you be perfect like Peter?" said Henry's mom every day.

As usual, Henry pretended not to hear. He continued melting Peter's crayons on the radiator.

But Horrid Henry started to think.

What if I were perfect? thought Henry. I wonder what would happen?

When Henry woke the next morning, he did not wake Peter by pouring water on Peter's head.

Peter did not scream.

This meant Henry's parents overslept, and Henry and Peter were late for Cub Scouts.

Henry was very happy.

Peter was very sad to be late for Cub Scouts.

But because he was perfect, Peter did not whine or complain.

On the way to Cub Scouts, Henry did not squabble with Peter over who sat in front. He did not pinch Peter and he did not shove Peter.

Back home, when Perfect Peter built a castle, Henry did not knock it down. Instead, Henry sat on the sofa and read a book.

Mom and Dad ran into the room.

"It's awfully quiet in here," said Mom. "Are you being horrid, Henry?"

"No," said Henry.

"Peter, is Henry knocking your castle down?"

Peter longed to say "Yes." But that would be a lie.

"No," said Peter.

He wondered why Henry was behaving so strangely.

"What are you doing, Henry?" said Dad.

"Reading a wonderful story about some super mice," said Henry.

Dad had never seen Henry read a book before. He checked to see if a comic book was hidden inside.

There was no comic book. Henry was actually reading a book.

"Hmmm," said Dad.

It was almost time for dinner. Henry was hungry and went into the kitchen, where Dad was cooking.

But instead of shouting "I'm starving! Where's my food?" Henry said, "Dad, you look tired. Can I help get supper ready?"

"Don't be horrid, Henry," said Dad, pouring peas into boiling water. Then he stopped.

"What did you say, Henry?" asked Dad.

"Can I help, Dad?" said Perfect Peter.

"I asked if you needed any help," said Henry.

"I asked first," said Peter.

"Henry will just make a mess," said Dad. "Peter, would you peel the carrots while I sit down for a moment?"

"Of course," said Perfect Peter.

Peter washed his spotless hands.

Peter put on his spotless apron.

Peter rolled up his spotless sleeves.

Peter waited for Henry to snatch the carrot peeler.

But Henry set the table instead.

Mom came into the kitchen.

"Smells good," she said. "Thank you, darling Peter, for setting the table. What a good boy you are."

Peter did not say anything.

"I set the table, Mom," said Henry.

Mom stared at him.

"You?" said Mom.

"Me," said Henry.

"Why?" said Mom.

Henry smiled.

"To be helpful," he said.

"You've done something horrid, haven't you, Henry?" said Dad.

"No," said Henry. He tried to look sweet.

"I'll set the table tomorrow," said Perfect Peter.

"Thank you, angel," said Mom.

"Dinner is ready," said Dad.

The family sat down at the table.

For dinner, they had spaghetti and meatballs with peas and carrots.

Henry ate his dinner with his knife and fork and spoon.

He did not throw peas at Peter and he did not slurp.

He did not chew with his mouth open and he did not slouch.

"Sit properly, Henry," said Dad.

"I am sitting properly," said Henry.

Dad looked up from his plate. He seemed surprised.

"So you are," he said.

Perfect Peter could not eat. Why wasn't Henry throwing peas at him?

Peter's hand reached slowly for a pea.

When no one was looking, he flicked the pea at Henry.

"Ouch," said Henry.

"Don't be horrid, Henry," said Mom.

Henry reached for a fistful of peas. Then Henry remembered he was being perfect and stopped.

Peter smiled and waited. But no peas bopped him on the head.

Perfect Peter did not understand. Where was the foot that always kicked him under the table?

Slowly, Peter stretched out his foot and kicked Henry.

"Ouch!" said Henry.

"Don't be horrid, Henry," said Dad.

"But I . . ." started Henry, but he stopped.

Henry's foot wanted to kick Perfect Peter around the block. Then Henry remembered he was being perfect and continued to eat.

"You're very quiet tonight, Henry," said Dad.

"The better to enjoy my lovely dinner," said Henry.

"Henry, where are your peas and carrots?" asked Mom.

"I ate them," said Henry. "They were delicious."

Mom looked on the floor. She looked under Henry's chair. She looked under his plate.

"You ate your peas and carrots?" said Mom slowly. She felt Henry's forehead. "Are you feeling all right, Henry?"

"Yeah," said Horrid Henry. "I'm fine. Thank you for asking," he added quickly.

Mom and Dad looked at each other. What was going on?

Then they looked at Henry.

"Henry, come here and let me give you a big kiss," said Mom. "You are a wonderful boy. Would you like a piece of fudge cake?"

Peter interrupted. "No cake for me, thank you," said Peter. "I would rather have more vegetables."

Henry let himself be kissed. Oh my, it was hard work being perfect.

He smiled sweetly at Peter.

"I would love some cake, thank you," said Henry.

Perfect Peter could stand it no longer. He picked up his plate and aimed at Henry.

Then Peter threw the spaghetti.

Henry ducked.

Splat!

The spaghetti landed on Mom's head. Tomato sauce trickled down her neck and down her new fuzzy pink jumper.

"PETER!!!!" yelled Mom and Dad.

"YOU HORRID BOY!" yelled Mom.

"GO TO YOUR ROOM!!" yelled Dad.

Perfect Peter burst into tears and ran to his room.

Mom wiped spaghetti off her face. She looked very funny.

Henry tried not to laugh. He squeezed his lips together tightly.

But it was no use. I am sorry to say that he could not stop a laugh from escaping.

"It's not funny!" shouted Dad.

"Go to your room!" shouted Mom.

But Henry didn't care.

Who would have thought being perfect would be such fun?

Chapter 2
HORRID HENRY'S DANCE CLASS

S̲tomp stomp stomp stomp stomp stomp stomp.

Horrid Henry was practicing his elephant dance.

Tap tap tap tap tap tap tap.

Perfect Peter was practicing his raindrop dance.

Peter was practicing being a raindrop for his class's dance recital.

Henry was also supposed to be practicing being a raindrop.

But Henry did not want to be a raindrop. He did not want to be a tomato, a string bean, or a banana, either.

Stomp stomp stomp went Henry's heavy boots.

Tap tap tap went Peter's tap shoes.

"You're doing it wrong, Henry," said Peter.

"No, I'm not," said Henry.

"You are, too," said Peter. "We're supposed to be raindrops."

Stomp stomp stomp went Henry's boots. He was an elephant smashing his way through the jungle and trampling on everyone who stood in his way.

"I can't concentrate with you stomping," said Peter. "And I have to practice my solo."

"Who cares?" screamed Horrid Henry. "I hate dancing, I hate dance class, and most of all, I hate you!"

This was not entirely true. Horrid Henry loved dancing. Henry danced in his bedroom. Henry danced up and down the stairs. Henry danced on the new sofa and on the kitchen table.

What Henry hated was having to dance with other children.

"Couldn't I go to karate instead?" asked Henry every Saturday.

"No," said Mom. "Too violent."

"Judo?" said Henry.

"N-O spells no," said Dad.

So every Saturday morning at 9:45 A.M., Henry and Peter's father drove them to Miss Impatience Tutu's Dance Studio.

Miss Impatience Tutu was skinny and bony. She had long, stringy gray hair. Her nose was sharp. Her elbows were pointy. Her knees were knobby. No one had ever seen her smile.

Perhaps this was because Impatience Tutu hated teaching.

Impatience Tutu hated noise.

Impatience Tutu hated children.

But most of all, Impatience Tutu hated Horrid Henry.

This was not surprising. When Miss Tutu shouted, "Class, lift your left legs," eleven left legs lifted. One right leg sagged to the floor.

When Miss Tutu screamed, "Heel, toe, heel,

toe," eleven dainty feet tapped away. One clumpy foot stomped toe, heel, toe, heel.

When Miss Tutu bellowed, "Class, skip to your right," eleven bodies turned to the right. One body galumphed to the left.

Naturally, no one wanted to dance with Henry. Or indeed, anywhere near Henry. Today's class, unfortunately, was no different.

"Miss Tutu, Henry is stepping on my toes," said Jeffrey.

"Miss Tutu, Henry is kicking my legs," said Linda.

"Miss Tutu, Henry is bumping me," said Camilla.

"*Henry!*" screeched Miss Tutu.

"Yeah," said Henry.

"I am a patient woman, and you are trying my patience to the limit," hissed Miss Tutu. "Any

more bad behavior and you will be very sorry."

"What will happen?" asked Horrid Henry eagerly.

Miss Tutu stood very tall. She took a long, bony finger and dragged it slowly across her throat.

Henry decided that he would rather live to do battle another day. He stood on the side, gnashing his teeth, pretending he was an enormous crocodile about to gobble up Miss Tutu.

"This is our final rehearsal before the show," barked Miss Tutu. "Everything must be perfect."

Eleven faces stared at Miss Tutu.

One face scowled at the floor.

"Tomatoes and beans to the front," ordered Miss Tutu.

"When Miss Thumper plays the music, everyone will stretch out their arms to the sky, to kiss the morning hello. Raindrops, stand at the back next to the giant green leaves and wait until the beans find the magic bananas. And, Henry," spat Miss Tutu, glaring. "Try to get it right.

"Positions, everybody. Miss Thumper, the opening music, please!" shouted Miss Tutu.

Miss Thumper banged away.

The tomatoes weaved in and out, twirling.

The beans pirouetted.

The bananas pointed their toes and swayed.

The raindrops pitter-patted. All except one. Henry waved his arms frantically and raced round the room. Then he crashed into the beans.

"Henry!" screeched Miss Tutu.

"Yeah," scowled Henry.

"Sit in the corner!"

Henry was delighted. He sat in the corner and made horrible rude faces while Peter did his raindrop solo.

Tap tap tap tap tap tap tap. Tappa tappa tappa tappa tap tap tap. Tappa tip tappa tip tappa tappa tappa tip.

"Was that perfect, Miss Tutu?" asked Peter.

Miss Tutu sighed. "Perfect, Peter, as

always," she said, and the corner of her mouth trembled slightly. This was the closest Miss Tutu ever came to smiling.

Then she saw Henry slouching on the chair. Her mouth drooped back into its normal grim position.

Miss Tutu tugged Henry off the chair. She shoved him to the very back of the stage, behind the other raindrops. Then she pushed him behind a giant green leaf.

"Stand there!" shouted Miss Tutu.

"But no one will see me here," said Henry.

"Precisely," said Miss Tutu.

It was showtime.

The curtain was about to rise.

The children stood quietly on stage.

Perfect Peter was so excited he almost bounced up and down. Naturally he controlled himself and stood still.

Horrid Henry was not very excited.

He did not want to be a raindrop.

And he certainly did not want to be a raindrop who danced behind a giant green leaf.

Miss Thumper waddled over to the piano. She
banged on the keys.

The curtain went up.

Henry's mom and dad were in the audience
with the other parents. As usual, they sat in the
back row, in case they had to make a quick get-
away.

They smiled and waved at Peter, who stood
proudly at the front.

"Can you see Henry?" whispered Henry's
mom to his dad.

Henry's dad squinted at the stage.

A tuft of red hair stuck up behind the green leaf.

"I think that's him behind the leaf," said his father doubtfully.

"I wonder why Henry is hiding," said Mom. "It's not like him to be shy."

"Hmmm," said Dad.

"Shhh," hissed the parents beside them.

Henry watched the tomatoes and beans searching on tiptoe for the magic bananas.

I'm not staying back here, he thought, and
pushed his way through the raindrops.

"Stop pushing, Henry!"
hissed Linda.

Henry pushed harder, then did a few pitter-
pats with the other raindrops.

Miss Tutu stretched out a bony arm and
yanked Henry back behind the scenery.

Who wants to be a raindrop anyway? thought
Henry. I can do what I like, hidden here.

The tomatoes weaved in and out, twirling.

The beans pirouetted.

The bananas pointed their toes and swayed.

The raindrops pitter-patted.

Henry flapped his arms and pretended he was a pterodactyl about to pounce on Miss Tutu.

Round and round he flew, homing in on his prey.

Perfect Peter stepped to the front and began his solo.

Tap tap tap tap tap tap . . . **CRASH!**

One giant green leaf fell on top of the raindrops, knocking them over.

The raindrops collided with the tomatoes.

The tomatoes smashed into the string beans.

The string beans bumped into the bananas.

Perfect Peter turned his head to see what was happening and then danced off the stage into the front row.

Miss Tutu fainted.

The only person still standing on stage was Henry.

Stomp stomp stomp stomp stomp stomp.

Henry did his elephant dance.

Boom boom boom boom boom boom.

Henry did his wild buffalo dance.

Peter tried to scramble back on stage.

The curtain fell.

There was a long silence, then Henry's parents clapped.

No one else did, so Henry's parents stopped.

All the other parents ran up to Miss Tutu and started shouting.

"I don't see why that horrid boy should have had such a long solo while all Linda did was lie on the floor," yelled one mother.

"My Jeffrey is a much better dancer than that boy," shouted another. "He should have done the solo."

"I didn't know you taught modern dance, Miss Tutu," said Camilla's mother. "Come, Camilla," she added, sweeping from the room.

"Henry!!" screeched Miss Tutu. "Leave my dance studio at once!"

"Whoopee!" shouted Henry. He knew that next Saturday he would be at karate class at last.

Chapter 3

HORRID HENRY AND MOODY MARGARET

"I'm Captain Hook!"

"No, I'm Captain Hook!"

"I'm Captain Hook," said Horrid Henry.

"I'm Captain Hook," said Moody Margaret.

They glared at each other.

"It's my hook," said Moody Margaret.

Moody Margaret lived next door.

She did not like Horrid Henry, and Horrid Henry did not like her. But when Joe was busy, and Toby had the flu, and Susan was her enemy, Margaret would jump over the wall to play with Henry.

"Actually, it's my turn to be Hook now," said Perfect Peter. "I've been the prisoner for such a long time."

"Prisoner, be quiet!" said Henry.

"Prisoner, walk the plank!" said Margaret.

"But I've walked it fourteen times already," said Peter. "Please, can I be Hook now?"

"No, by thunder!" said Moody Margaret. **"Now out of my way, worm!"** And she swashbuckled across the deck, waving her hook and clutching her sword.

Margaret had eye patches, skulls and crossbones, plumed hats and cutlasses, swords and daggers.

Henry had a stick.

This was why Henry played with Margaret.

But Henry had to do terrible things before

playing with Margaret's swords. Sometimes he had to sit and wait while she read a book.

Sometimes he had to play "House" with her. Worst of all (please don't tell anyone), he sometimes had to be the baby.

Henry never knew what Margaret would do.

When he put a spider on her arm, Margaret laughed.

When he pulled her hair, Margaret pulled his harder.

When Henry screamed, Margaret would scream louder. Or she would sing. Or pretend not to hear.

Sometimes Margaret was fun. But most of the time she was a moody old grouch.

"I won't play if I can't be Hook," said Horrid Henry.

Margaret thought for a moment.

"We can both be Captain Hook," she said.

"But we only have one hook," said Henry.

"Which I haven't played with yet," said Peter.

"Be quiet, prisoner!" shouted Margaret. "Mr. Smee, take him to jail."

"No," said Henry.

"You will get your reward, Mr. Smee," said the Captain, waving her hook.

Mr. Smee dragged the prisoner to the jail.

"If you're very quiet, prisoner, then you will be freed and you can be a pirate, too," said Captain Hook.

"Now give me the hook," said Mr. Smee.

The Captain reluctantly handed it over.

"Now I'm Captain Hook and you're Mr. Smee," shouted Henry. "I order everyone to walk the plank!"

"I'm sick of playing pirates," said Margaret. "Let's play something else."

Henry was furious. That was just like Moody Margaret.

"Well, I'm playing pirates," said Henry.

"Well, I'm not," said Margaret. "Give me back my hook."

"No," said Henry.

Moody Margaret opened her mouth and screamed. Once Margaret started screaming she could go on and on and on.

Henry gave her the hook.

Margaret smiled.

"I'm hungry," she said. "Got anything good to eat?"

Henry had three bags of chips and seven chocolate chip cookies hidden in his room, but he certainly wasn't going to share them with Margaret.

"You can have a radish," said Henry.

"What else?" said Margaret.

"A carrot," said Henry.

"What else?" said Margaret.

"Glop," said Henry.

"What's Glop?"

"Something special that only I can make," said Henry.

"What's in it?" asked Margaret.

"That's a secret," said Henry.

"I bet it's yucky," said Margaret.

"Of course it's yucky," said Henry.

"I can make the yuckiest Glop of all," said Margaret.

"That's because you don't know anything. No one can make yuckier Glop than I can."

"I dare you to eat Glop," said Margaret.

"I double-dare you back," said Henry. "Dares go first."

Margaret stood up very straight.

"All right," said Margaret. "Glop starts with snails and worms."

And she started poking under the bushes.

"Got one!" she shouted, holding up a fat snail.

"Now for some worms," said Margaret.

She got down on her hands and knees and started digging a hole.

"You can't put anything from outside into

Glop," said Henry quickly. "Only stuff from the kitchen."

Margaret looked at Henry.

"I thought we were making Glop," she said.

"We are," said Henry. "My way, because it's my house."

Horrid Henry and Moody Margaret went into the gleaming white kitchen. Henry got out two wooden mixing spoons and a giant red bowl.

"I'll start," said Henry. He went to the cupboard and opened the doors wide.

"Oatmeal!" said Henry. And he poured some into the bowl.

Margaret opened the fridge and looked inside. She grabbed a small container. "Soggy noodles!" shouted Margaret. Into the bowl it went.

"Coleslaw!"

"Spinach!"

"Coffee!"

"Yogurt!"

"Flour!"

"Vinegar!"

"Baked beans!"

"Mustard!"

"Peanut butter!"

"Moldy cheese!"

"Pepper!"

"Rotten oranges!"

"And ketchup!" shouted Henry. He squirted in the ketchup until the bottle was empty.

"Now mix!" said Margaret.

Horrid Henry and Moody Margaret grabbed hold of their spoons with both hands. Then they plunged the spoons into the Glop and began to stir.

It was hard, heavy work. Faster and faster, harder and harder they stirred.

There was Glop on the ceiling. There was Glop on the floor. There was Glop on the clock, and Glop on the door. Margaret's hair was covered in Glop. So was Henry's face.

Margaret looked into the bowl. She had never seen anything so yucky in her life.

"It's ready," she said.

Horrid Henry and Moody Margaret carried the Glop to the table.

Then they sat down and stared at the **sloppy, slimy, sludgy, sticky, smelly, gooey, gluey, gummy, greasy, gloopy Glop.**

"Right," said Henry. "Who's going to eat some first?"

There was a very long pause.

Henry looked at Margaret.

Margaret looked at Henry.

"Me," said Margaret. "I'm not scared."

She scooped up a large spoonful and stuffed it in her mouth. Then she swallowed. Her face went pink and purple and green.

"How does it taste?" asked Henry.

"Good," said Margaret, trying not to choke.

"Have some more then," said Henry.

"Your turn next," said Margaret.

Henry sat for a moment and looked at the Glop.

"My mom doesn't like me to eat between meals," said Henry. *"Henry!"* hissed Moody Margaret. Henry took a tiny spoonful.

"More!" said Margaret.

Henry took a tiny bit more. The Glop wobbled lumpily on his spoon. It looked like— Henry did not want to think about what it looked like. He closed his eyes and brought the spoon to his mouth.

"Ummm, yummm," said Henry.

"You didn't eat any," said Margaret. "That's not fair."

She scooped up some Glop and . . .

I dread to think what would have happened next, if they had not been interrupted.

"Can I come out now?" called a small voice from outside. "It's my turn to be Hook."

Horrid Henry had forgotten all about Perfect Peter.

"Okay," shouted Henry.

Peter came to the door.

"I'm hungry," he said.

"Come in, Peter," said Henry sweetly. "Your dinner is on the table."

Chapter 4

HORRID HENRY'S VACATION

Horrid Henry hated vacations.

Henry's idea of a super vacation was sitting on the sofa eating chips and watching TV.

Unfortunately, his parents usually had other plans.

Once they took him to see a castle. But there was no castle. There were only piles of stones and broken walls.

"Never again," said Henry.

The next year he had to go to a lot of museums.

"Never again," said Mom and Dad.

Last year they went to the beach.

"The sun is too hot," Henry muttered.

"The water is too cold," Henry whined.

"The food is yucky," Henry grumbled.

"The bed is lumpy," Henry moaned.

This year they decided to try something different.

"We're going camping in France," said Henry's parents.

"Hooray!" said Henry.

"You're happy, Henry?" said Mom. Henry had never been happy about any vacation plans before.

"Oh yes," said Henry. Finally, finally, they were doing something good.

Henry knew all about camping from Moody Margaret. Margaret had been camping with her family. They had stayed in a big tent with comfy

beds, a fridge, a stove, a bathroom, a shower, a heated swimming pool, a disco, and a great big giant TV with fifty-seven channels.

"Oh boy!" said Horrid Henry.

"Bonjour!" said Perfect Peter.

The great day arrived at last. Horrid Henry, Perfect Peter, Mom, and Dad boarded the ferry for France.

Henry and Peter had never been on a boat before.

Henry jumped on and off the seats.

Peter did a lovely drawing.

The boat went up and down, and up and down.

Henry ran back and forth between the aisles.

Peter pasted stickers in his notebook.

The boat went up and down, and up and down.

Henry sat on a revolving chair and spun around.

Peter played with his puppets.

The boat went up and down, and up and down.

Then Henry and Peter ate a big greasy lunch of burgers and fries in the café.

The boat went up and down, and up and down, and up and down.

Henry began to feel queasy.

Peter began to feel queasy.

Henry's face went green.

Peter's face went green.

"I think I'm going to be sick," said Henry, and threw up all over his mom.

"I think I'm going to be—" said Peter, and threw up all over his dad.

"Oh no," said Mom.

"Never mind," said Dad. "I just know this will be our best vacation ever."

Finally, the boat arrived in France.

After driving and driving and driving, they finally reached the campsite.

It was even better than Henry's dreams. The tents were as big as houses. Henry heard the happy sound of TVs blaring, music playing, and children splashing and shrieking. The sun was shining. The sky was blue.

"Wow, this looks great," said Henry.

But the car drove on.

"Stop!" said Henry. "You've gone too far."

"We're not staying in that awful place," said Dad.

They drove on.

"Here's our campsite," said Dad. "A real campsite!"

Henry stared at the bare rocky ground under the cloudy grey sky.

There were three small tents flapping in the wind. There was a single faucet. There were a few trees. There was nothing else.

"It's wonderful!" said Mom.

"It's wonderful!" said Peter.

"But where's the TV?" said Henry.

"No TV here, thank goodness," said Mom. "We've got books."

"But where are the beds?" said Henry.

"No beds here, thank goodness," said Dad. "We've got sleeping bags."

"But where's the pool?" said Henry.

"No pool," said Dad. "We'll swim in the river."

"Where's the toilet?" said Peter.

Dad pointed at a distant cubicle. Three people stood waiting.

"All the way over there?" said Peter. "I'm not complaining," he added quickly.

Mom and Dad unpacked the car. Henry stood and scowled.

"Who wants to help put up the tent?" asked Mom.

"I do!" said Dad.

"I do!" said Peter.

Henry was horrified. "We have to put up our own tent?"

"Of course," said Mom.

"I don't like it here," said Henry. "I want to go camping in the other place."

"That's not camping," said Dad. "Those tents have beds in them. And bathrooms. And showers. And fridges. And stoves, and TVs. Horrible." Dad shuddered.

"Horrible," said Peter.

"And we have such a lovely, snug tent here," said Mom. "Nothing modern—just wooden pegs and poles."

"Well, I want to stay there," said Henry.

"We're staying here," said Dad.

"No!" screamed Henry.

"Yes!" screamed Dad.

I am sorry to say that Henry then had the longest, loudest, noisiest, shrillest, most horrible tantrum you can imagine.

Did you think that a horrid boy like Henry would like nothing better than sleeping on hard, rocky ground in a soggy sleeping bag without a pillow?

You thought wrong.

Henry liked comfy beds.

Henry liked crisp sheets.

Henry liked hot baths.

Henry liked microwave dinners, TV, and noise.

He did not like cold showers, fresh air, and quiet.

Far off in the distance the sweet sound of loud music drifted toward them.

"Aren't you glad we're not staying in that awful noisy place?" said Dad.

"Oh yes," said Mom.

"Oh yes," said Perfect Peter.

Henry pretended he was a bulldozer come to knock down tents and squash campers.

"Henry, don't barge the tent!" yelled Dad.

Henry pretended he was a hungry Tyrannosaurus rex.

"Ow!" shrieked Peter.

"Henry, don't be horrid!" yelled Mom.

She looked up at the dark cloudy sky.

"It's going to rain," said Mom.

"Don't worry," said Dad. "It never rains when I'm camping."

"The boys and I will go and collect some more firewood," said Mom.

"I'm not moving," said Horrid Henry.

While Dad made a campfire, Henry played his boom box as loud as he could, stomping in time to the terrible music of the Killer Boy Rats.

"Henry, turn that noise down this minute," said Dad.

Henry pretended not to hear.

"Henry!" yelled Dad. ***"Turn that down!"***

Henry turned the volume down the teeniest, tiniest fraction.

The terrible sounds of the Killer Boy Rats continued to boom over the quiet campsite.

Campers emerged from their tents and shook their fists. Dad switched off Henry's tape player.

"Anything wrong, Dad?" asked Henry, in his sweetest voice.

"No," said Dad.

Mom and Peter returned carrying armfuls of firewood.

It started to drizzle.

"This is fun," said Mom, slapping a mosquito.

"Isn't it?" said Dad. He was heating up some tins of baked beans.

The drizzle turned into a downpour.

The wind blew.

The campfire hissed and went out.

"Never mind," said Dad brightly. "We'll eat our baked beans cold."

Mom was snoring.

Dad was snoring.

Peter was snoring.

Henry tossed and turned. But whichever way he turned in his damp sleeping bag, he seemed to be lying on sharp, pointy stones.

Above him, mosquitoes buzzed.

I'll never get to sleep, he thought, kicking Peter. How am I going to stand this for fourteen days?

Around four o'clock on the fifth day, the family huddled inside the cold, damp, smelly tent listening to the howling wind and the pouring rain.

"Time for a walk!" said Dad.

"Great idea!" said Mom, sneezing. "I'll get the boots."

"Great idea!" said Peter, sneezing. "I'll get the slickers."

"But it's pouring outside," said Henry.

"So?" said Dad. "What better time to go for a walk?"

"I'm not coming," said Horrid Henry.

"I am," said Perfect Peter. "I don't mind the rain."

Dad poked his head outside the tent.

"The rain has stopped," he said. "I'll remake the fire."

"I'm not coming," said Henry.

"We need more firewood," said Dad. "Henry can stay here and collect some. And make sure it's dry."

Henry poked his head outside the tent. The rain had stopped, but the sky was still cloudy. The fire spat.

I won't go, thought Henry. The forest will be all muddy and wet.

He looked around to see if there was any wood closer to home. That was when he saw the thick, dry, wooden pegs holding up all the tents.

Henry looked to the left.

Henry looked to the right.

No one was around.

If I just take a few pegs from each tent, he thought, they'll never be missed.

When Mom and Dad came back they were delighted.

"What a lovely roaring fire," said Mom.

"Clever of you to find some dry wood," said Dad.

Henry dreamed he was floating in a cold river, floating, floating, floating.

He woke up. He shook his head. He was floating. The tent was filled with cold muddy water.

Then the tent collapsed on top of them.

Henry, Peter, Mom, and Dad stood outside in

68

the rain and stared at the river of water gushing through their collapsed tent.

All around them were soaking wet campers staring at their collapsed tents.

Peter sneezed.

Mom sneezed.

Dad sneezed.

Henry coughed, choked, spluttered, and sneezed.

"I don't understand it," said Dad. "This tent never collapses."

"What are we going to do?" said Mom.

"I know," said Henry. "I've got a very good idea."

Two hours later Mom, Dad, Henry, and Peter were sitting on a sofa-bed inside a tent as big as a house, eating chips and watching TV.

The sun was shining. The sky was blue.

"Now this is what I call a vacation!" said Henry.

HA HA

HEE HEE

If you don't have milk coming out of your nose yet, you're not laughing hard enough!

The two newest L.A.F. books are sure to make you chuckle, giggle, and guffaw!*

FUNNY BOY MEETS THE AIRSICK ALIEN FROM ANDROMEDA

What do you do when a big, purple, smelly alien threatens to eat up Earth? Tell him a joke, of course.

Well, that's what Funny Boy thinks. He's the latest (and greatest?) joke-telling superhero and he's here to rescue Earth from the airsick alien from Andromeda. He's not strong. He can't fly. Equipped with only a (bad) sense of humor, Funny Boy's going to save the day. We hope . . .

LAB COAT GIRL AND THE AMAZING BENJAMIN BONE

When Trudie and Benjamin get together, something strange always happens. So when the two are paired up for a class project, Trudie is sure that crazy things will occur. And they do! Join Trudie as she tries to solve the mysteries that surround Benjamin Bone.

IN BOOKSTORES OCTOBER 1999

A. F. :) Part of a well-balanced meal!

*This message is brought to you by RCABF: "Reading Can Actually Be Funny."

WHAT THE HECK DOES

L.A.F.

TELL US AND WIN!

STAND FOR?

THE FUNNIEST, SIDE·SPLITTIN' ENTRIES WIN!

GRAND PRIZE:

Your entry will be featured in L.A.F. book #5 and you will receive a signed copy of book #3

10 RUNNERS UP:

Receive a copy of L.A.F. book #3 signed by the author

YES! Enter me in the "What the Heck Does L.A.F. Stand For?" contest

I THINK L.A.F. SHOULD STAND FOR...

L: **A:**   **F:**

Name: Birthdate:

Address:

City: State: Zip:

To enter, visit **WWW.LAFBOOKS.COM** or send entry form to L.A.F. Contest c/o Hyperion Books for Children, 114 Fifth Ave., Room 1411C, New York, NY 10011